This book was written to educate and aware people about the dangers of sex trafficking. Sex trafficking is very relevant in society and shouldn't be ignored. Social media has allowed online predators to prey on victims manipulating them into devastating situations.

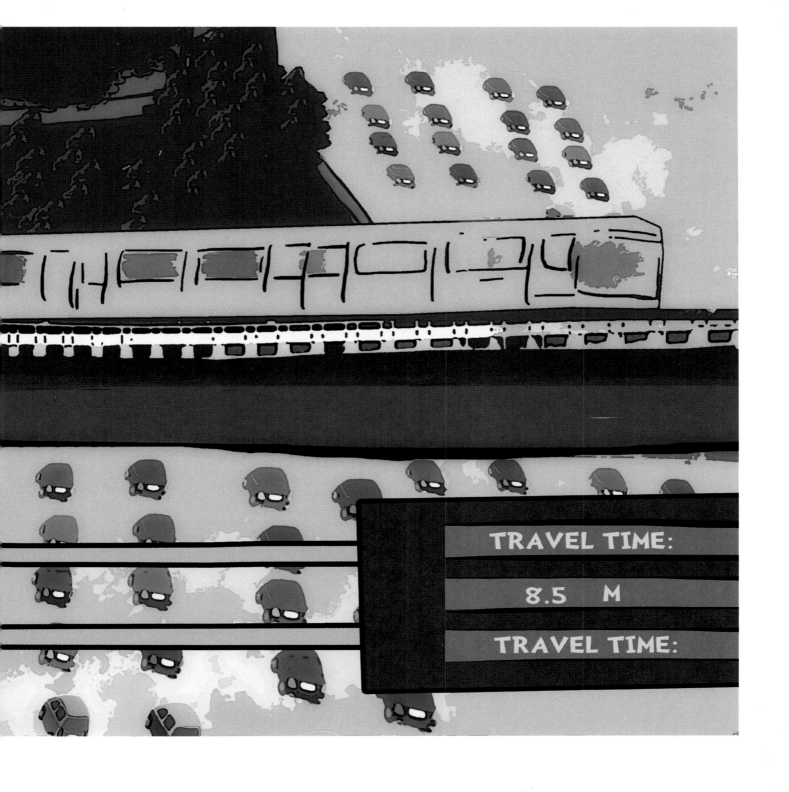

The Blakes live in an upscale neighborhood in Atlanta Georgia.

The Blake family consists of Mr. and Mrs. Blake and their two daughters Deniece and Yolanda.

Mr. Blake owns a mechanic shop in North Atlanta.

THE MECHANIC SHOP

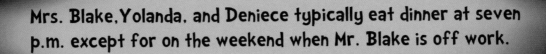

Mrs. Blake, Yolanda, and Deniece typically eat dinner at seven p.m. except for on the weekend when Mr. Blake is off work.

Yolanda frequently chats with different people on social media.

While on social media Yolanda connects with a guy name Jeff.

While washing the dishes Yolanda sends Jeff a text message, "My daddy is getting on my nerves."

Jeff sends Yolanda a text message to meet him later to have some fun.

Yolanda agrees to meet Jeff.

Yolanda agrees to meet Jeff at a Park near her house.

While her parents are sleeping Yolanda escapes through her bedroom window.

When Yolanda arrives at the park Jeff isn't there.
Yolanda sends Jeff a text message "WYA."

Jeff replies to Yolanda's text message "I'm near the stop sign."

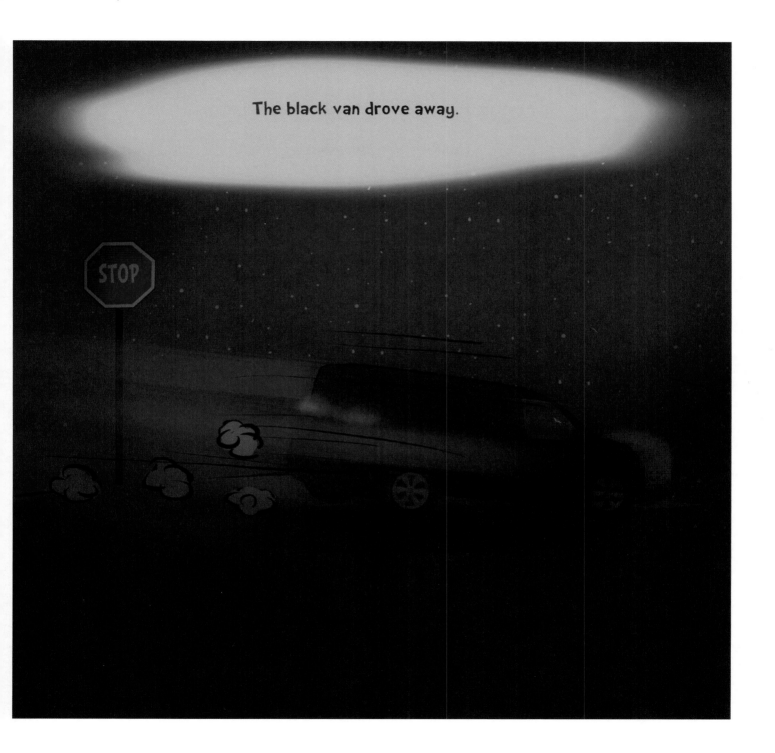

The police officers arrive at the Blake's residence.
I haven't seen Yolanda since yesterday.
POLICE
Mr. Blake files a missing persons report for Yolanda with the police.

A week has gone by and Yolanda is still missing.
I hope Yolanda is Ok.
I miss my sister...

The police issue a city wide search for Yolanda.

The police receive   an anonymous tip about Yolanda.

Yolanda was last seen in the Fulton Industrial area located in Southwest Atlanta.

The police check out the tip to see if it is valid.

Many people in the area confirm that Yolonda was seen with Terry.

The police asked the people in the neighborhood to call if they see Terry in the area.

The police received a tip that Terry was recently seen in the Fulton Industrial area.

While entering the room the police officers discover Yolanda with two other girls.

The police arrested Terry.

Terry was charged and convicted of sex trafficking. Terry was sentenced to twenty years in Federal Prison.

Yolanda and the girls are lucky to be alive. Many girls get coerced and manipulated in thinking they are meeting a companion through casual conversation on social media. Unfortunately, there are predators who search the internet preying on young vulnerable girls who seek attention. Sex trafficking is a serious problem that plagues society.

www.rashadpatterson.com

What is Sex Trafficking?

It is the illegal transportation of people from one area to another for sexual exploitation.

What is a Sex Trafficker?

A person who is involved in the illegal movement of people from one area to another for sexual exploitation.

Where does Sex Trafficking take place?

Sex trafficking can take place in many different places including fake massage parlors, city streets, truck stops, strip clubs, and hotels.

Glossary

Anonymous - a person who is not identified by name.

Cat fishing - to entice a person into a relationship through a fake profile.

Confirm - to establish the truth.

Chat - to communicate online in a friendly way.

Escape - to break free from control.

Sex trafficking - is illegally transporting people from one area to another for sexual manipulation.

Social Media - Websites and application that allow people to connect socially online.

Thank you for taking the opportunity to purchase and read my book I really appreciate it.

RASHAD PATTERSON

www.rashadpatterson.com

Hook: Runaway Girl Ain't no Love in the Streets
       Love in the Streets / Love in the Streets
       Runaway Girl Ain't no Love in the Streets
       Love in the Streets / Love in the Streets
       In these Streets

Verse: She learned out the hard way the streets don't Love you
Mommy and Daddy them the ones that love you
It's an Underworld beneath the Underworld
Turned her bitter now she a sour little girl
Got caught up in a life that she didn't know exist
The person she connect with didn't exist
It a network of wolves trying to get money
Its predators out here they ain't sparing you for the money
Better listen to your parents they ain't gone stir you wrong
The wrong turn is the wrong turn
Cause the outcome is long term
Be aware of your surrounding and who you connect with
Cause everybody ain't meant to connect with
Seems all good but it went left quick
They put her to work on F.I.B.
Cars stopping and honking on F.I.B.
Now she trapped in da life on F.I.B.

Made in the USA
Columbia, SC
17 January 2020